Barnaby Is Not Afraid of Anything

Gilles Bizouerne / *Illustrated by* **Béatrice Rodriguez**

Princeton Architectural Press · New York

With a white and black muzzle,
cozied up in his favorite red-and-white striped scarf,
Barnaby is a badger.

And Barnaby doesn't take any risks.

But one evening, after the rain, Barnaby meets
his friends, Constance the turtle and Claire the mole.

The trio decides to take a moonlight walk.

Beside a puddle, they discover some strange footprints.
"Odd! I've never seen these prints before," says Constance.

"You think that it's a dinovore?" Claire asks.

"We say *dinosaur*," Barnaby explains. "But it can't be, the prints are too small..."

The friends decide to keep going.

They are not afraid of anything and venture out a little further.

"Stop!" says Constance. "The footprints lead to that hut over there! Who wants to go and see?"

“I-I’m going to
stay here,” Claire
stammers.

“I’ll go,” Barnaby bravely
declares. “If you hear me
scream, come and help me!”

Softly on tippy toes, Barnaby approaches the hut. *Platch, Plotch! Platch, Plotch!*

Suddenly, he sees a shadow…
…with a very long nose!

Oh no! Barnaby is a little scared!
He quickly runs away and joins his friends.
Plapotch, Plapotch, Plapotch!

"I saw someone!" Barnaby shares, out of breath.
"He has a very long nose!"
"A very long nose?" Claire repeats. "Oh no! Maybe it's a witch?"

“Impossible!” Constance calls out. “Witches don’t exist. I will go and see.”
“Be careful,” says Barnaby.

Softly, on tippy toes, Constance approaches the hut. *Platch, Plotch! Platch, Plotch!*

She sees a hunched-over shadow with a very long nose and long, skinny fingers.

Oh no! Constance is a little scared!
She quickly runs away and joins her friends.
Plapotch, Plapotch, Plapotch!

“There’s someone in there!” cries Constance.
“With a very long nose and…long, skinny fingers and a hunchback!”

"Oh brother!" Barnaby frets. "We better go home."

Constance puffs out of her chest. "Out of the question! We can't give up!"

"Claire, where are you going?"

"Claiiiire?"

Claire rubs her eyes. "I hid…
And then I fell asleep."

"We need you," Barnaby says
encouragingly. "It's your turn
to go and see."

But Constance shakes
her head. "No, she is
too small."

Now Claire stands up a little taller.
"Not at all. I am big too!
I already brush my teeth all by
myself. I'll go."

And on the softest and tippiest of toes, Claire approaches the hut.
Platch, Plotch! Platch, Plotch!

Barnaby and Constance watch for Claire's return.
After a while, they begin to worry!

“What do we do?” asks Constance.
“We have no choice,” Barnaby replies. “Let’s go.”

As the friends approach, Claire leans out of the hut. “Come closer! It’s not a witch! His name is Gideon, and he is a hero.”

"*Heron*," Gideon corrects, amused.
"I made a long trip from a very chilly country, and I rested here as the rain passed."

"Of course, it all makes sense now!" Barnaby exclaims. "The strange prints in the mud are the traces of your feet."

"In the night, we took your beak for a long nose…"

"…and your bundle for a hunchback!"

Gideon laughs. “What an imagination!”
“We weren’t afraid at all!” says Constance.
“We’re super brave,” explains Claire.
“Like knights,” adds Barnaby.

As they wave goodbye to Gideon, Barnaby laughs.
"Tomorrow, we will sleep under the stars!"